PUPPY TALES Too!

by Hans Wilhelm

Scholastic Reader — Level 1

SCHOLASTIC INC. Cartwheel B·O·O·K·S ®

New York   Toronto   London   Auckland   Sydney
Mexico City   New Delhi   Hong Kong   Buenos Aires

I Love My Shadow! (0-439-33210-9). Copyright © 2002 by Hans Wilhelm, Inc.
No Kisses, Please! (0-439-56420-4). Copyright © 2004 by Hans Wilhelm, Inc.
I Can Help! (0-439-46621-0). Copyright © 2003 by Hans Wilhelm, Inc.
I Hate Bullies! (0-439-70139-2). Copyright © 2005 by Hans Wilhelm, Inc.
I'm Not Scared! (0-439-44334-2). Copyright © 2002 by Hans Wilhelm, Inc.
I Hate Bedtime! (0-439-68264-9). Copyright © 2004 by Hans Wilhelm, Inc.

All rights reserved. Published by Scholastic Inc. SCHOLASTIC, CARTWHEEL BOOKS, and associated logos are trademarks and/or registered trademarks of Scholastic Inc.

12 11 10 9 8 7 6 5 4 3 2 1   5 6 7 8 9 10

This edition created exclusively for Barnes & Noble, Inc.
2005 Barnes & Noble Books
ISBN 0-7607-9510-X

Printed in the USA   24

This edition first printing, May 2005

I LOVE MY SHADOW!

by Hans Wilhelm

I am going to the beach.

Look!
I brought a friend.

I like to chase him.

But sometimes
he chases me.

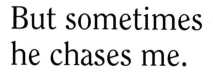

He can be short and fat.

But sometimes
he is very tall and thin.

My friend can be
very funny.

And sometimes he can be
a little scary.

But he always likes
to play with me.

Oh, no!
Here comes
a big cloud.

Now my friend
is gone.

I am all alone.

I know what to do!

I chase the cloud away!

Now my friend is back again.

We are a great team.

NO KISSES, PLEASE!

NO KISSES, PLEASE!

by Hans Wilhelm

I hear a car!
We have a visitor.

Who can it be?

Oh, no.

It's Auntie Judy!

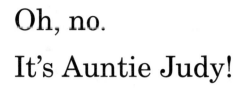

She always kisses me.

I hate kisses.
I must hide.

Now I am safe.

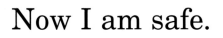

There you are.
I found you!

Oh, no!

HELLLLLP!

What should I do?

I have an idea!

I dig a hole.

Now you can kiss me.

It worked!
No kisses.

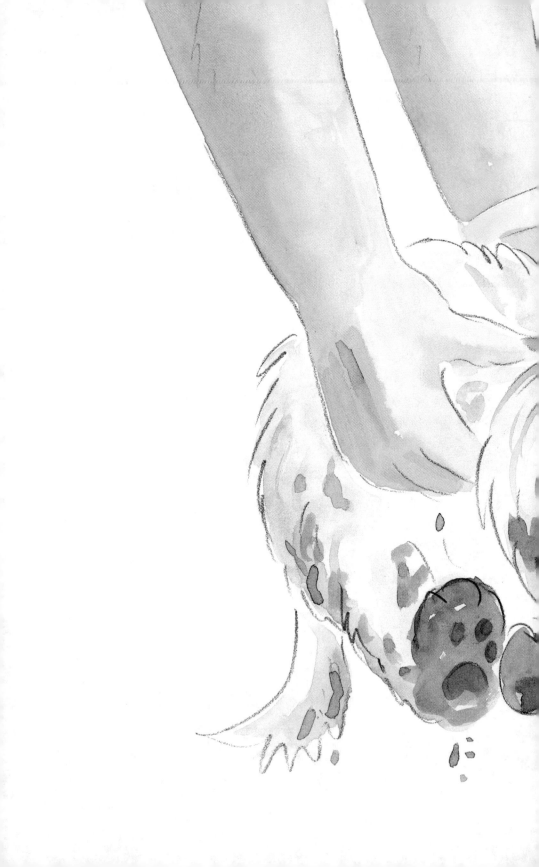

Oh, no. What now?

Baths are better than kisses.

I CAN HELP!

I CAN HELP!

by Hans Wilhelm

Today, I play grown-up.

I can help Baby.

Oops!

I can help clean.

Oh, no!

I can help plant.

Oops!

I can't do anything.
I'm useless.

Why are grown-ups so smart?

They must have made
many mistakes, too.

They just didn't quit.
And neither will I!

Come here, Baby.
Let me help you.

I am very careful.

See? I can help!

Boom!

I HATE BULLIES!

I HATE BULLIES!

by Hans Wilhelm

Look what I have.

Go away! This is MY bone.

HELP!

I am safe.

It's good to be small.

Oh, no!
The gate is open.

Let go of my bone!

I hate bullies.

This is not fair.

I have an idea!

Turn on the hose.

Here we go!

Run, Bully, run!

I got my bone back.

I will eat it inside.

I'M NOT SCARED!

I'M NOT SCARED!

by Hans Wilhelm

It's Halloween!
It's time to dress up.

What should I be?

Maybe I should be a funny
clown with big feet.

Should I be a bad, bad pirate . . .

or a barking robot?

Maybe I'll be a
big, black bat.

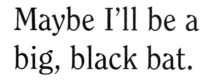

Should I be a scary wolf . . .

or a cute little
bunny?

Do you like me as
a silly, slimy sea serpent?

Should I be a wise wizard . . .

or an orange pumpkin?

Maybe I should be a mummy.

I know! I will be Super Dog,
and I'll save the world.

Uh-oh! What is this?

Oh, no!

I am scared
of ghosts.

But these are not
real ghosts!

These are my friends!
They are here to play!

Next year I'll give
THEM a scare!

I HATE BEDTIME!

I HATE BEDTIME!

by Hans Wilhelm

I'm not tired.

I hate bedtime.

I will stay up and play.

It's too dark
to go outside.

I'll play with Cat.

Cat is sleeping.

Baby is sleeping, too.

Everyone is sleeping.

I have an idea!

Here's a slipper.

Let's go!

Whee!
What fun!

Oh, no!

Crash!

I'm very sleepy now.